# Beneath th

### By Chris Do

**Cover Artist:** David Griffith • **Editor:** Tim Wadzinski

**Interior Artists:** Chris Yarbrough

**Cartographer:** Keith Curtis • **Design:** Edward Lavallee

**Interior Layout:** Jamie Wallis

### Visit us online at:
### www.goodman-games.com

Get digital updates and corrections free! Use the coupon code below on this title at www.rpgnow.com to receive a free digital copy of this module plus any updated editions as they are published.

### 3eb86a

---

This printing of Fifth Edition Fantasy #14: Beneath the Keep is done under version 1.0 of the Open Gaming License, and the System Reference Document by permission from Wizards of the Coast, Inc. Designation of Product Identity: The following items are hereby designated as Product Identity in accordance with Section 1(e) of the Open Game License, version 1.0: Fifth Edition Fantasy #14: Beneath the Keep, all proper nouns, capitalized terms, italicized terms, artwork, maps, symbols, depictions, and illustrations, except such elements that already appear in the System Reference Document or have been released as Open Content.

Designation of Open Content: Subject to the Product Identity designation above, such sections of creature and NPC statistics as derive from the SRD are designated as Open Gaming Content.

Some of the portions of this book which are delineated OGC originate from the System Reference Document and are copyright © 1999, 2000 Wizards of the Coast, Inc. The remainder of these OGC portions of these book are hereby added to Open Game Content and, if used, should bear the COPYRIGHT NOTICE "Fifth Edition Fantasy #14: Beneath the Keep, copyright © 2018 Goodman Games, all rights reserved, visit www.goodman-games.com or contact info@goodman-games.com"

Fifth Edition Fantasy #14: Beneath the Keep is copyright © 2018 Goodman Games. Open game content may only be used under and in the terms of the Open Game License.

Goodman Games is not affiliated with Wizards of the Coast™. Goodman Games makes no claim to or challenge to any trademarks held by Wizards of the Coast™.

OPEN GAME LICENSE Version 1.0a

The following text is the property of Wizards of the Coast, Inc. and is Copyright 2000 Wizards of the Coast, Inc ("Wizards"). All Rights Reserved.

1. Definitions: (a)"Contributors" means the copyright and/or trademark owners who have contributed Open Game Content; (b)"Derivative Material" means copyrighted material including derivative works and translations (including into other computer languages), potation, modification, correction, addition, extension, upgrade, improvement, compilation, abridgment or other form in which an existing work may be recast, transformed or adapted; (c) "Distribute" means to reproduce, license, rent, lease, sell, broadcast, publicly display, transmit or otherwise distribute; (d)"Open Game Content" means the game mechanic and includes the methods, procedures, processes and routines to the extent such content does not embody the Product Identity and is an enhancement over the prior art and any additional content clearly identified as Open Game Content by the Contributor, and means any work covered by this License, including translations and derivative works under copyright law, but specifically excludes Product Identity. (e) "Product Identity" means product and product line names, logos and identifying marks including trade dress; artifacts; creatures characters; stories, storylines, plots, thematic elements, dialogue, incidents, language, artwork, symbols, designs, depictions, likenesses, formats, poses, concepts, themes and graphic, photographic and other visual or audio representations; names and descriptions of characters, spells, enchantments, personalities, teams, personas, likenesses and special abilities; places, locations, environments, creatures, equipment, magical or supernatural abilities or effects, logos, symbols, or graphic designs; and any other trademark or registered trademark clearly identified as Product identity by the owner of the Product Identity, and which specifically excludes the Open Game Content; (f) "Trademark" means the logos, names, mark, sign, motto, designs that are used by a Contributor to identify itself or its products or the associated products contributed to the Open Game License by the Contributor (g) "Use", "Used" or "Using" means to use, Distribute, copy, edit, format, modify, translate and otherwise create Derivative Material of Open Game Content. (h) "You" or "Your" means the licensee in terms of this agreement.

2. The License: This License applies to any Open Game Content that contains a notice indicating that the Open Game Content may only be Used under and in terms of this License. You must affix such a notice to any Open Game Content that you Use. No terms may be added to or subtracted from this License except as described by the License itself. No other terms or conditions may be applied to any Open Game Content distributed using this License.

3. Offer and Acceptance: By Using the Open Game Content You indicate Your acceptance of the terms of this License.

4. Grant and Consideration: In consideration for agreeing to use this License, the Contributors grant You a perpetual, worldwide, royalty-free, non-exclusive license with the exact terms of this License to Use, the Open Game Content.

5. Representation of Authority to Contribute: If You are contributing original material as Open Game Content, You represent that Your Contributions are Your original creation and/or You have sufficient rights to grant the rights conveyed by this License.

6. Notice of License Copyright: You must update the COPYRIGHT NOTICE portion of this License to include the exact text of the COPYRIGHT NOTICE of any Open Game Content You are copying, modifying or distributing, and You must add the title, the copyright date, and the copyright holder's name to the COPYRIGHT NOTICE of any original Open Game Content you Distribute.

7. Use of Product Identity: You agree not to Use any Product Identity, including as an indication as to compatibility, except as expressly licensed in another, independent Agreement with the owner of each element of that Product Identity. You agree not to indicate compatibility or co-adaptability with any Trademark or Registered Trademark in conjunction with a work containing Open Game Content except as expressly licensed in another, independent Agreement with the owner of such Trademark or Registered Trademark. The use of any Product Identity in Open Game Content does not constitute a challenge to the ownership of that Product Identity. The owner of any Product Identity used in Open Game Content shall retain all rights, title and interest in and to that Product Identity.

8. Identification: If you distribute Open Game Content You must clearly indicate which portions of the work that you are distributing are Open Game Content.

9. Updating the License: Wizards or its designated Agents may publish updated versions of this License. You may use any authorized version of this License to copy, modify and distribute any Open Game Content originally distributed under any version of this License.

10. Copy of this License: You MUST include a copy of this License with every copy of the Open Game Content You Distribute.

11. Use of Contributor Credits: You may not market or advertise the Open Game Content using the name of any Contributor unless You have written permission from the Contributor to do so.

12. Inability to Comply: If it is impossible for You to comply with any of the terms of this License with respect to some or all of the Open Game Content due to statute, judicial order, or governmental regulation then You may not Use any Open Game Material so affected.

13. Termination: This License will terminate automatically if You fail to comply with all terms herein and fail to cure such breach within 30 days of becoming aware of the breach. All sublicenses shall survive the termination of this License.

14. Reformation: If any provision of this License is held to be unenforceable, such provision shall be reformed only to the extent necessary to make it enforceable.

15 COPYRIGHT NOTICE

Open Game License v 1.0 Copyright 2000, Wizards of the Coast, Inc.

System Rules Document Copyright 2000 Wizards of the Coast, Inc.; Authors Jonathan Tweet, Monte Cook, Skip Williams, based on original material by E. Gary Gygax and Dave Arneson.

Fifth Edition Fantasy #14: Beneath the Keep, copyright © 2018 Goodman Games, all rights reserved, visit www.goodman-games.com or contact info@goodman-games.com

# BENEATH THE KEEP

## By Chris Doyle

Beneath the Keep is an adventure designed for use with the 5th edition of the first fantasy roleplaying game. It is intended for four to six 1st-level characters and can be completed in a single session. A variety of character classes is suggested to tackle the challenges of solving the murder mystery presented herein. A cleric would be very beneficial to overcome several of the undead challenges, and silvered or magic weapons are crucial to have a chance against the final foe. The adventure is set in several finished chambers and natural caves below a remote keep or outpost, and can easily be dropped into a similar setting or a more urban location of the GM's own design.

## BACKGROUND

Situated in the wilderness is a fortified keep, sitting atop a natural flat-top hill. The keep is a bastion of good people, eking out an existence in the untamed wilds, but surrounded by evil on all sides. Thick stone walls patrolled by able-bodied men-at-arms provide protection to a thriving community. Roving bands of bloodthirsty humanoids, ravenous wild beasts, and vile brigands are but a few of the constant threats that face the inhabitants of the keep. Even from beneath the very foundation of the keep do the forces of evil oppose the good folk residing within.

Garan is a simple man, the proprietor of a small provision shop located in the wilderness keep. He sells all manner of mundane items such as cookery and building supplies, and adventuring equipment such as rope, flasks of oil, and backpacks. Although a few spears and long knives are for sale in the shop, Garan sends those seeking arms and armor to a nearby blacksmith. His prices are fair, and he is always interested in tales from beyond the wall, or is quick to offer his pessimistic view on the local leadership. Garan lives alone in a small apartment at the back of his shop, unaware that a secret door conceals passage to a long-forgotten cellar. But agents of evil are aware of those secret underground chambers, and use them to further their nefarious plots in the region.

A few miles from the keep is a hidden temple of unspeakable evil and ultimate chaos. The secluded sanctuary is dedicated to a foul deity of chaos, manned by an active congregation of foul priests and acolytes. The god requires frequent blood sacrifices to appease and grant its followers evil spells. This requires a steady supply of captives and slaves, which the local bandits (and sometimes humanoids) are more than willing to provide—for a price. The easiest source of these slaves is the keep, a popular stop-over for travelers, adventurers, and merchants.

Illyana Tatranova is one of the agents of chaos, a former acolyte that succumbed to the curse of lycanthropy while questing in her god's name. She came to the hidden temple a few years ago and pledged her service. Due to her curse, she was never truly accepted by the clerical hierarchy and often was outright shunned. Attracted to the hustle and the bustle of the nearby keep, it was a natural landing spot. She soon discovered the natural honeycomb of caves beneath the keep, and a few finished chambers under Garan's shop, apparently long-forgotten. These chambers were a perfect hideout, complete with an abandoned shrine, a winding escape route, and plenty of monstrous rats.

Today, she is an agent, spy, and slaver for the nearby temple of chaos. Using stealth and her ability to assume the form of a rat, she gathers information on easy targets visiting the keep (those that would not go missing). Using trained carrier pigeons, she communicates with local bandits on target appearance, group composition, and departure/arrival schedules. Once captured by the bandits, captives are transported to the nearby temple of chaos for eventual sacrifice. The bounty paid to the bandits is shared with Illyana, although her motivation is less material wealth, and more for the thrill of the mark, and the devotion to serve her dark god.

But last night, by chance Garan located the secret door in his apartment (installed by the previous owner for his own nefarious motives), and cautiously crept down the stairs to a dusty cellar. He triggered a trap on the stairs set by Illyana, which summoned her rat allies to investigate. She had no choice but to slaughter the fool before he fled back up the stairs to summon the night watch. She hastily staged a murder scene in the shop, and moved the body deeper into her lair, before pondering her next move. Not willing to so easily give up her lair, she prepares for an eventual investigation.

## ADVENTURE HOOKS

This adventure begins with the characters already present at the wilderness keep. It's up to the GM to decide why the characters are at the keep, and how they can get involved in the investigation of a missing local shopkeeper. A few suggestions are presented.

- The characters are hired by a friend or family member of Garan to investigate his disappearance. The patron lacks confidence that the garrison troops can or will conduct a comprehensive investigation.

- The characters are getting ready to embark on a wilderness adventure, and head to the provisioner's shop early in the morning to pick up a few supplies needed for overland travel. Once there, they encounter the town guard, who have sealed off the shop as a crime scene. Since the town guard have little appetite to conduct an investigation, the natural curiosity of the characters gets the best of them, and they look into the matter.

- The night before, the characters get in trouble with the local authorities, likely while carousing at the local tavern. To pay for damages, or avoid legal action, the characters agree to investigate the crime scene.

**Quest: Investigate Garan's Disappearance and Bring the Responsible Party to Justice.** Regardless of the hook used, the characters' goal is to investigate Garan's disappearance, and determine Illyana's motivation and connection with the hidden temple of chaos. Depending on the hook used, the GM needs to determine what an appropriate award (if any) would be for the completion of this task.

## BEGINNING THE ADVENTURE

The adventure begins when the characters agree to investigate an obvious crime scene. Read or paraphrase the text below, adjusting the text based on the particular hook employed by the GM:

*As you approach the provisions shop, you are greeted by a gathering of town guard. Two guards stand at attention, blocking entrance to the shop door with a pair of crossed spears. The morning sun glints off their shiny helmets. Several other guards, adorned in chain mail and carrying halberds, mill about, most of them looking bored. Another guard, wearing plate armor, appears to be in charge, and is questioning a portly man in priestly garb.*

If the characters interact with the guards, they are motioned to talk to the corporal of the watch (the guard wearing plate armor). Assuming the characters agree to investigate the crime scene, continue with the description of area 1.

## GENERAL FEATURES

**The Shop.** Areas 1 and 2 are above ground, located in the courtyard of the wilderness keep. The building is constructed of stout timbers with a peaked slate roof. A single locked wooden Dutch-style door provides access to the shop. Garan had the only key. The door can be forced open with a successful DC 20 Strength (Athletics) check, or can be unlocked with a successful DC 22 Dexterity check using thieves' tools. A guard is fetching a master key from the garrison. The door is AC 15 and has 20 hit points. The building has but one story with a 10-foot-high ceiling. There are two small windows, one of them smashed open (see area 1 for details).

**Finished Chambers.** Areas 3 through 7 are all about 30 feet below ground. These chambers are dusty but mostly dry. Areas 4 and 7 see quite a bit of traffic from Illyana and her rat allies. Areas 5 and 6 have gone unused for many years and are coated with a thick layer of dust. The walls of these chambers are smooth hewn stone, with ceilings averaging 8 to 12 feet high unless otherwise noted. Climbing one of these walls requires a successful DC 17 Strength (Athletics) check.

**Natural Caverns.** Area 8 is a set of twisting passages, created by water flow through soft limestone. The passages gradually slope east to west. These walls are damper, and vary in width (typically 3 to 7 feet) and height (typically 6 to 8 feet, unless otherwise noted in the text). These walls sport many interesting flowstone structures and the occasional stalactite or stalagmite. The floor is uneven, and strewn with small rubble and scree. The walls are easier to scale, requiring a successful DC 13 Strength (Athletics) check to climb.

FIFTH EDITION FANTASY • BENEATH THE KEEP

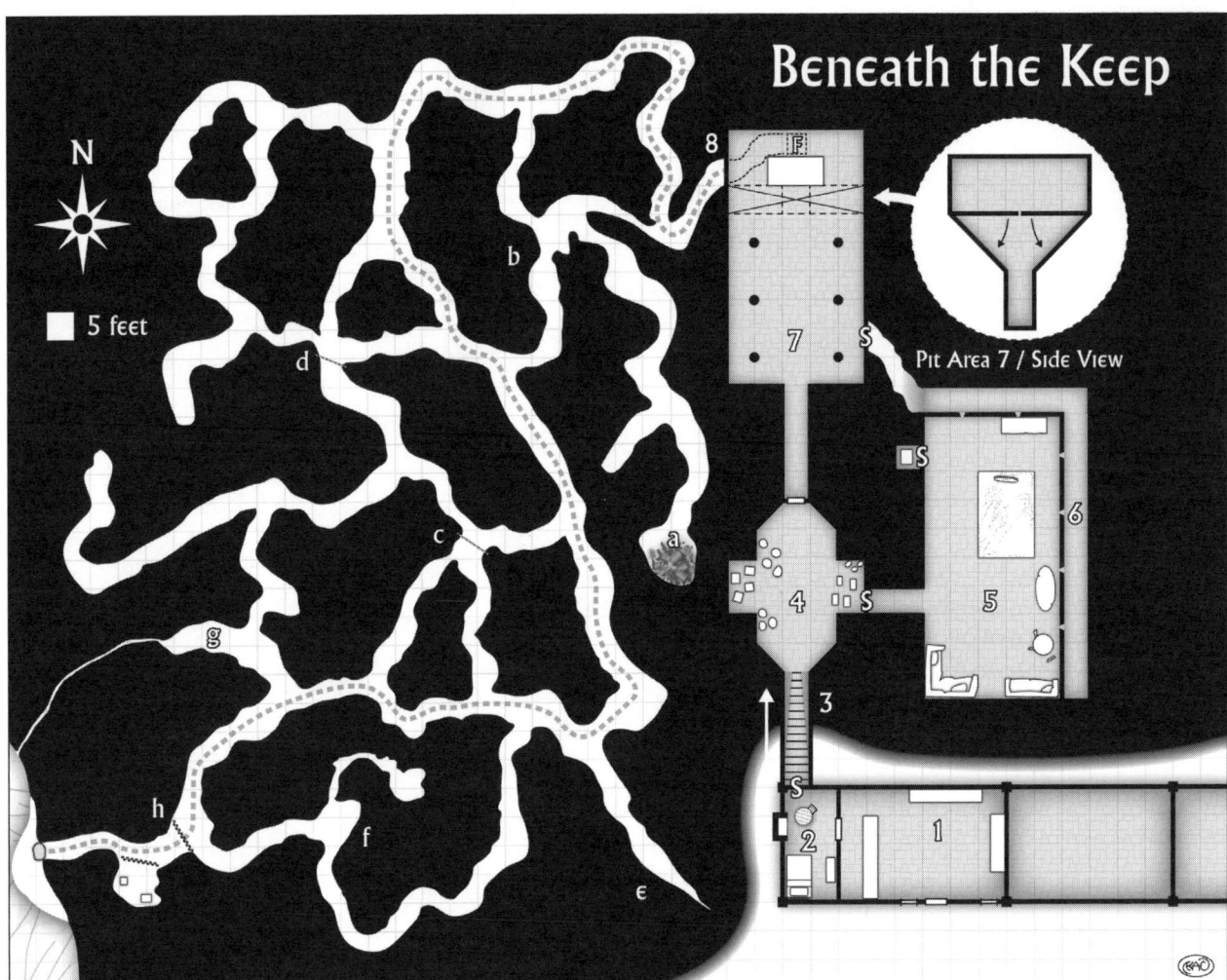

## AREA 1 – THE SHOP

Read or paraphrase the following:

*The door to the shop opens to reveal a mess. Flanking the entrance are a pair of windows, one of which is smashed. Wooden shelf units are tumbled to the floor, some even splintered beyond repair. Slashed packs, tangled rope, and mundane supplies are strewn about the floor in a chaotic morass. The shop is about 30 feet wide and 20 feet deep, with dark paneled walls. To the left, a wooden counter runs the length of the room. Behind the counter is a closed wooden door.*

This interior room was the provisioner's shop. The provisioner sold mostly mundane items and typical adventuring gear. Such items include cookery, lanterns, rope, packs, blankets, and simple tools (hammers and saws). Three spears and five long knives (treat as daggers) are the only weapons present, although a successful DC 15 Intelligence (Investigation) check reveals a small leather pouch holding eight silver ball bearings that could be used as sling bullets.

It has since been ransacked by Illyana to make it look like someone broke in (via the smashed window), and that person was looking for something. But there are several clues to raise suspicion that the ransacking was staged. These include:

- **Smashed Window.** Examination of the broken window reveals that the glass shards are mostly outside the shop, indicating it was smashed from the inside. It was indeed broken from the interior, which can be discerned with a successful DC 13 Intelligence (Investigation) check.

- **Lock Box.** Under the counter is a battered metal lockbox, still sealed. The box is locked (Garan had the only key), but it can be picked with a successful DC 18 Dexterity check using thieves' tools. Inside the box are 37 sp and 12 gp.

- **Valuables.** Each successful DC 10 Intelligence (Investigation) check following a full minute of searching reveals a valuable item still present. These items include an electrum-handled magnifying glass (worth 120 gp), a teak box holding a variety of inks with fancy quills (worth 65 gp), a crystal vial of fancy perfume (worth 25 gp), and an obsidian orb (an arcane focus; worth 20 gp).

FIFTH EDITION FANTASY • BENEATH THE KEEP

- **Door.** The door to area 2 has been forced, although it's closed. A successful DC 15 Intelligence (Investigation) check reveals it has been forced from area 2 to 1. Illyana did not have the key to the door, and needed to force it to gain access to the shop to stage the ransacking.

## AWARDING EXPERIENCE

For each clue that the characters uncover, divide 25 XP among them.

## AREA 2 – GARAN'S APARTMENT

When the characters enter this room from area 1, read or paraphrase the following:

*The door opens to reveal a cozy studio apartment, about 20 feet wide by 10 feet deep. The floor is covered with a plush but worn oval-shaped carpet. Opposite the door, behind a battered round wooden table and chair, is a soot-stained hearth. To its left, a simple bed with disheveled sheets is pushed into the corner. To the left of the door is a writing desk although it lacks a chair. On the desk rests a square box-like object concealed under a stained cloth sheet.*

This room served as the simple living quarters for Garan. The bed, desk, table, and chair are all nondescript. Stuffed in the mattress is a leather pouch with a gold thread drawstring (worth 22 gp). Inside the pouch are 24 sp, 10 gp, and an uncut emerald (worth 100 gp). The carpet, although in dire need of cleaning, would fetch 15 gp. Next to the hearth is a small pile of firewood, and several well-used pots and pans.

A small wooden cage, about 3 feet on each side, is hidden under the cloth on the table. The cage holds a **wing-clipped cockatrice** Garan recently acquired from a merchant that needed hard coin to settle a gambling debt. Illyana discovered this oddity while staging the break-in. She unlatched the cage, so the magical beast could escape with ease, but until now, it had little reason to do so. If a character removes the covering, the startled fowl bursts out of the cage, attacking with surprise. The mistreated beast flops around the chamber, attacking targets at random. The wing-clipped cockatrice fights to the death.

**Secret Cache.** Under the carpet is a loose flagstone that conceals a secret hollow that Garan was unaware of. This hollow was constructed by the previous owner of the shop, and can be located with a DC 20 Wisdom (Perception) check. Inside is a locked metal box, the single key long lost. The lock can be picked with a successful DC 14 Dexterity check using thieves' tools. Inside the box is a pouch holding seven garnets (each worth 50 gp), a *+1 dagger* in an electrum accented black leather scabbard (worth 75 gp), and a scrimshaw scroll tube with a whale motif (worth 135 gp). The tube contains a treasure map (left to the GM to design), and a map depicting the construction of the underground chambers below this shop. This crudely sketched map displays the secret door to area 3, area 4, the secret doors to areas 5 and 6, and area 7. Using this map, the depicted secret doors can be automatically found.

**The Way Down.** The secret door located on the north wall can be discovered with a successful DC 20 Wisdom (Perception) check. The door is opened by releasing a secret catch near the floor, and then pushing inward. A DC 12 Intelligence (Investigation) check reveals a smear of blood on the wall, near one seam of the secret door. This smear was made by Garan as he fled up the stairs clutching a dagger wound, before Illyana caught up to him and finished the deed. If this smear is located, the Wisdom (Perception) check to find the secret door is made with advantage.

## WING-CLIPPED COCKATRICE

*Small monstrosity, unaligned*

**AC:** 11

**Hit Points:** 21 (6d6)

**Speed:** 20 ft.

| STR | DEX | CON | INT | WIS | CHA |
|---|---|---|---|---|---|
| 6 (-2) | 14 (+2) | 10 (+0) | 2 (-4) | 13 (+1) | 5 (-3) |

**Senses:** darkvision 60 ft., passive perception 11

**Languages:** -

**Challenge:** 1/2 (100 XP)

### ACTIONS

**Bite:** *Melee Weapon Attack:* +4 to hit, reach 5 ft., one creature. *Hit:* 4 (1d4 + 2) piercing damage and the target must succeed on a DC 11 Constitution saving throw against being magically petrified. On a failed save, the creature begins to turn to stone and is restrained. It must repeat the saving throw at the end of its next turn. On a success, the effect ends. On a failure, the creature is petrified for 24 hours.

*About the size of a housecat, this twisted creature sports the traits of a scaly lizard complete with a whip-like tail, a bat, and fowl. It appears to once have had wings, but instead leathery nubs are present. Its sinewy neck has odd patches of black and gray feathers.*

## AWARDING EXPERIENCE

If the characters defeat the wing-clipped cockatrice, divide 100 XP among them. If the characters find the secret cache, divide 50 XP among them.

## AREA 3 – TRAPPED STAIRS

When the characters find the secret door in area 2, continue reading or paraphrase the following:

*The secret door opens to reveal a stone stairway descending into the inky darkness.*

The original owner of the shop had the underground chambers constructed, and included a trap on these stone steps. The seventh step down is made of wood, and when 25 or more pounds of weight is placed on it, it shifts to a steep incline. A creature that triggers this trap must make a DC 15 Dexterity saving throw, or slip and tumble down to the bottom of the stairs. The fall causes 3 (1d6) bludgeoning damage and the target is prone at the base of the steps. If a character descending the steps is tapping with a spear or 10-foot pole, the trap is automatically discovered as the wooden step is hollow. Otherwise, a DC 15 passive Wisdom (Perception) check is required to discover the trap before it's too late.

Illyana is aware of the trap, and makes sure it is set at all times. She has also added her own twist, since Garan found the secret door recently. On the bottom step, she has placed a clay urn, about 3 feet high. She has weakened the exterior of the urn with a few careful hammer blows. Inside the urn is a **green slime** (Dungeon Master's Guide, p. 105), collected from area 8b. A target tumbling down the steps automatically careens into the urn, which causes it to shatter and release the small colony of green slime. The target takes 3 (1d6) acid damage at the start of each of its turns until the slime is scraped off or destroyed. If the trap is not triggered and the characters simply examine the urn by opening it, a DC 10 Dexterity saving throw is needed to avoid the slime's attack.

## AWARDING EXPERIENCE

If the characters avoid the trapped steps and the green slime in the urn, divide 50 XP between them.

## AREA 4 – CELLAR

After the characters reach the bottom of the stairs and deal with the trap, read or paraphrase the following:

*The air is cooler and damp, with slight staleness. At the base of the steps is a shadowy chamber with smooth walls and a smooth ceiling about 8 feet high. The chamber expands to 15 feet wide and stretches for at least 30 feet or so. Through the gloom, there appears to be a stone door on the opposite side of the chamber. Several empty torch sconces adorn the walls. The east and west walls each sport a recessed niche about 10 feet wide, piled high with crates and casks. You catch a glimpse of movement from between the stacked crates, and soon several sets of beady, glowing eyes peer from around the crates.*

This chamber is an old cellar, used to this day as storage and serving no other purpose than to grant access to the rooms beyond. The crates (there are 12) contain a variety of old mundane items, such as torches, moth-eaten blankets, earthenware plates, and the like. Most items are worthless. The casks (there are 10) are either empty (75% chance) or contain stale water. One cask holds a few rotting haunches of meat. This is used by Illyana to slip past the cave moray in area 8f.

Illyana expects the town guard to investigate the disappearance of Garan eventually, so she commanded six **giant blight rats** (from area 8a) to guard this chamber. The giant blight rats are hungry and don't even attempt to hide among the crates. Shortly after the characters arrive, they close in to attack. Somewhat slower than a typical giant rat, but heartier, the giant blight rats attempt to maneuver into position to utilize their Pack Tactics trait. They fight to the death since the door to area 7 is sealed.

**Secret Door.** Hidden in the eastern niche behind a pile of crates is a secret door that can be located with a successful DC 17 Wisdom (Perception) check. The door can be pushed open following pulling down a nearby torch sconce. Beyond the door is a short 5-foot-wide passage that leads to area 5.

## GIANT BLIGHT RAT (6)

*Small beast, unaligned*

**AC:** 11

**Hit Points:** 9 (2d6 + 2)

**Speed:** 30 ft.

| STR | DEX | CON | INT | WIS | CHA |
|---|---|---|---|---|---|
| 7 (-2) | 13 (+1) | 13 (+1) | 2 (-4) | 10 (+0) | 4 (-3) |

**Senses:** darkvision 60 ft., passive perception 10

**Languages:** -

**Challenge:** 1/8 (25 XP)

**Keen Smell:** The giant blight rat has advantage on Wisdom (Perception) checks that rely on smell.

**Pack Tactics:** The giant blight rat has advantage on an attack roll against a creature if at least one of the giant blight rat's allies is within 5 feet of the creature and the ally isn't incapacitated.

### ACTIONS

**Bite:** *Melee Weapon Attack:* +3 to hit, reach 5 ft., one target. *Hit:* 3 (1d4 + 1) piercing damage. If the target is a creature, it must succeed on a DC 10 Constitution saving throw or contract a disease. After an onset of 12 hours, and until the disease is cured, the target suffers disadvantage on all Dexterity-based attacks and saving throws from muscle fatigue and soreness. The target's maximum hit points are reduced by 2 (1d4) every 24 hours, and hit points can only be regained via magical means. If the target's hit point maximum drops to 0 as the result of this blight, the target dies.

*These monstrous rodents are about 3 feet long, not counting their black hairless whip-like tails. They have pale gray fur, matted and dirty, and yellow beady eyes.*

## AWARDING EXPERIENCE

For each giant blight rat the characters defeat, divide 25 XP among them. If the characters find the secret door, divide 50 XP among them.

## AREA 5 – ABANDONED GAMBLING PARLOR

If the characters discover this hidden chamber, read or paraphrase the following:

*The air here is drier and a thick coat of dust coats the chamber. The chamber is about 50 feet by 25 feet. A once plush red carpet covers the floor, although now it decays and is tattered in places. The smooth stone walls are covered with once fancy tapestries, now faded, unravelling, and drooping. To the right are several rotting remains of comfortable sofas and divans, their fabric torn and stuffing poking out in places. The crumbled piles of several small wooden tables are located among the sofas. To the left, a large stone table about 15 feet long dominates the open floor. A dust-covered horizontal wheel of chance rests on the stony surface, among several other items, perhaps chips or coins.*

The carpet, rotting tapestries, and sofas were all once elegant and valuable. But now, time has rendered them worthless. The previous owner of the shop had these chambers constructed, and secluded an illegal gambling parlor in the cellars. In this chamber, he would host all manner of games of chance, often for high stakes, with friends but also rivals and enemies. Hence the secret passage (area 6) that allowed his allies to spy while he "entertained." The peepholes are concealed into the wall, and require a successful DC 25 Wisdom (Perception) check to locate.

On the table is an assortment of coins (13 cp and 22 sp), along with 50 clay chips marked in a variety of denominations (1, 5, 10, and 50). The wheel is constructed from black oak and is adorned with lapis lazuli (worth 50 gp), but it weighs 30 pounds and is somewhat fragile.

One of these enemies, particularly fond of gambling, still resides in this chamber cursed for all eternity. Following a night of bad luck, a wizard rival attempted to skip town before settling his debt. He was captured and sealed alive in the stone "table." In a cruel twist of fate, he was entombed with a few *spell scrolls* of offensive weapons to aid in taking his own life. But instead he slowly suffocated, and since his soul was so corrupted and evil, his corpse never rotted fully, and he was cursed to an undead state, forever forced to listen to others having enjoyment winning (or losing) on bets. To this day, he is an abomination known as a **zombire**: a zombie that still has limited use of the arcane arts. But he is still sealed inside the "table."

To open the stone table (which is similar to a sarcophagus) the east side needs to be examined with a successful DC 17 Wisdom (Perception) check. This reveals a series of four small "buttons" that can be depressed. If depressed in the correct sequence, which takes three successive Intelligence (Investigation) checks of DC 13, DC 15, and DC 17, the table lid becomes unlocked. Then it merely requires a DC 12 Strength (Athletics) check to lift or slide the lid off. Of course, the zombire has been waiting for decades for his chance to escape, and gladly assists with this task!

The zombire does not waste an action getting out of the table, using its interior as half cover. He unleashes a barrage of spells on his enemies. He starts with a *ray of sickness* and then a *witch bolt* on a fighter-type until he drops. He saves *false life* until it's needed, and then relies on cantrips, being most fond of *chill touch*. Insulted by the inclusion of the scrolls, he refuses to use them and fights until destroyed.

Aside from the moldering remains of his robes, there are two scroll tubes in the table. One holds a *spell scroll* of *burning hands*, while the second holds a *spell scroll* of *chromatic orb*.

**Secret Closet.** In the west wall is a secret door that conceals a secure closet used to hold winnings. It can be found with a successful DC 20 Wisdom (Perception) check. Note that this secret door is not depicted on the map found in area 2. Once a hidden release is tripped near the ceiling, the stone door can be slid to the right, revealing a 5-foot-by-5-foot closet. Inside are several rotten wooden shelves that have since collapsed. Among the rotten timbers is a pile of assorted coins (111 sp, 13 ep, 47 gp) and several gems. These include three pieces of jet (each worth 25 gp), a piece of amber (50 gp), a yellow topaz (100 gp), and an aquamarine (100 gp). A gold ring set with obsidian (worth 225 gp) can also be located in the mess with a successful DC 14 Wisdom (Perception) check.

# ZOMBIRE

*Medium undead, neutral evil*

**AC:** 8

**Hit Points:** 22 (3d8 + 9)

**Speed:** 20 ft.

| STR | DEX | CON | INT | WIS | CHA |
|---|---|---|---|---|---|
| 11 (+0) | 6 (-2) | 16 (+3) | 12 (+1) | 6 (-2) | 5 (-3) |

**Saving Throws:** Wisdom +0

**Damage Immunities:** poison

**Condition Immunities:** poisoned

**Senses:** darkvision 60 ft., passive perception 8

**Languages:** Common

**Challenge:** 1 (200 XP)

**Innate Spellcasting:** The zombire's innate spellcasting ability is Intelligence (spell save DC 11, +3 to hit with spell attacks). The zombire can innately cast the following spells, requiring no verbal or material components:

- At will: *chill touch, mage hand, ray of frost*
- 1/day each: *false life, ray of sickness, witch bolt*

**Undead Fortitude:** If damage reduces the zombire to 0 hit points, it must make a Constitution saving throw with a DC of 5 + the damage taken, unless the damage is radiant or from a critical hit. On a success, the zombire drops to 1 hit point.

## ACTIONS

**Slam:** *Melee Weapon Attack:* +2 to hit, reach 5 ft., one target. *Hit:* 3 (1d6) bludgeoning damage.

*Dry gray flesh is tightly wrapped over the bones of this humanoid creature. Its frame is clad in tattered robes, and glowing red eyes pierce from the folds of a rotting hood. As it wordlessly conjures arcane energy, it points a crooked finger.*

## AWARDING EXPERIENCE

If the characters defeat the zombire, divide 200 XP among them. If the characters find the secret closet, divide 50 XP among them.

## AREA 6 – SECRET PASSAGE

This secret passage can be accessed from the secret door in area 7. A 5-foot-wide corridor runs along the north and east walls of the gambling parlor. Six eye-level (about 5 feet off the floor) peepholes are in the corridor, to allow easy spying on those in area 5. There are four such peepholes on the east wall and two along the north wall. If used, a creature in area 5 needs to succeed on a DC 14 passive Perception check to notice the spying.

At the GM's discretion, Illyana can be in this corridor and she takes the opportunity to spy on the characters. While the characters explore the parlor (perhaps if they discover the secret of the stone table), she casts *necrotic wave* through a peephole on as many targets as possible, attempting to soften up her foes before an eventual confrontation. Shortly after, she hastens to area 7 to make a stand behind the altar there.

## AREA 7 – TEMPLE

When the characters enter this chamber, read or paraphrase below:

*The corridor ends at an archway to a large chamber, with a 20-foot-high ceiling. The room is about 25 feet wide and extends at least 40 feet into the distance. The floor is smooth fitted flagstones, and the walls are plain and unadorned. Three sets of columns spaced equidistant lead to the far end of the hall, where a black altar rests. Dark metal candelabras flank the altar holding blood-red unlit candles.*

This chamber is an ancient temple, since repurposed by Illyana to reflect her dark god of chaos. Here she worships and performs rites to appease her god, so he continues to grant her spells for her to serve his nearby congregation. The columns go all the way up to the ceiling and provide half cover. A secret door is located on the east wall that conceals passage to area 6. It can be found with a successful DC 18 Wisdom (Perception) check. It is clearly depicted on the map found in area 2. There is no lock; it simply requires brute force to be placed along the correct pressure point to slide the door inward.

A concealed pit trap is located in front of the altar, 5 feet wide, but stretching the full 25 feet from wall to wall. It can be discovered with a successful DC 15 Wisdom (Perception) check. The pit is 10 feet deep, but only the 5-foot-by-5-foot center. A fall here causes 3 (1d6) points of bludgeoning damage, but a fall anywhere else along the pit does not cause damage as the bottom is an inclined plane that deposits a target into the deep center of the pit. See the cross-section of this trap on the map for clarity. However, a **swarm of skeletal rats** inhabits the pit, and attacks any creatures that fall in. The swarm spills out of the pit to attack if the trap is triggered.

The candelabras, shaped like serpentine hydras, are each worth 65 gp, and the candles (12 total) are each worth 10 gp. The altar is a solid block of black granite. On the floor behind the altar is a hidden trapdoor that can be discovered with a successful DC 13 Wisdom (Perception) check. Several metal rungs lead down to a natural corridor that heads west to area 8.

Crouching behind the altar, awaiting the characters, is **Illyana Tatranova, wererat acolyte**. Before long, she stands up and openly mocks them. She uses the altar as half cover, and attempts to goad them into triggering the pit trap. She has likely already used one of her 1st-level spell slots in area 6, so she is cautious about using spells. She could cast another *necrotic wave* to soften up a group of foes, but she would prefer to save one slot for *command*. She tries to get a target to blunder back into the pit with a *command* of "Flee." She casts *shield of faith* if melee looks inevitable. Otherwise, she resorts to throwing daggers, keeping one in reserve for melee. If reduced to 8 or fewer hit points, she uses an action to toss her *elemental shard* (which releases a **fire mephit**), and then she flees down the trapdoor, escaping to area 8. Using her knowledge of the natural caverns and their dangers, she hopes to escape the characters' clutches and flee to the nearby temple in the wilderness.

## SWARM OF SKELETAL RATS

*Medium swarm of Tiny undead, lawful evil*

**AC:** 12 (natural armor)
**Hit Points:** 31 (7d8)
**Speed:** 30 ft.

| STR | DEX | CON | INT | WIS | CHA |
|---|---|---|---|---|---|
| 9 (-1) | 11 (+0) | 11 (+0) | 2 (-4) | 10 (+0) | 3 (-4) |

**Damage Resistances:** piercing, slashing
**Condition Immunities:** charmed, exhaustion, frightened, paralyzed, petrified, poisoned, prone, restrained, stunned
**Senses:** darkvision 60 ft., passive perception 10
**Languages:** -
**Challenge:** 1/4 (50 XP)

**Swarm:** The swarm can occupy another creature's space and vice versa, and the swarm can move through any opening large enough for a Tiny rat. The swarm can't regain hit points or gain temporary hit points.

### ACTIONS

**Bite:** *Melee Weapon Attack:* +2 to hit, reach 0 ft., one target in the swarm's space. *Hit:* 7 (2d6) piercing damage, or 3 (1d6) piercing damage if the swarm has half of its hit points or fewer.

*The pit holds a writhing mass of bleach-white skeletal rodents, each with oversized black incisors and glowing pinpoints of unholy light in empty eye sockets. As the mass belches forth, the unnerving cracking and snapping of bones announces its movements.*

## ILLYANA TATRANOVA, WERERAT ACOLYTE

*Medium humanoid (human, shapechanger), lawful evil*

**AC:** 13 (leather armor)
**Hit Points:** 27 (6d8)
**Speed:** 30 ft.

| STR | DEX | CON | INT | WIS | CHA |
|---|---|---|---|---|---|
| 10 (+2) | 14 (+2) | 10 (+0) | 11 (+0) | 14 (+1) | 10 (+0) |

**Saving Throws:** Wisdom +4, Charisma +2
**Skills:** Perception +4, Stealth +4
**Damage Immunities:** bludgeoning, piercing, and slashing damage from nonmagical attacks not made with silvered weapons
**Senses:** darkvision 60 ft. (rat form only), passive perception 14
**Languages:** Common (can't speak in rat form)
**Challenge:** 2 (450 XP)

**Special Equipment:** Illyana wears leather armor and a bronze holy symbol, and carries six daggers (one with a tiny opal set in pommel worth 120 gp), the key to the padlock in area 8h, and an *elemental shard* (see appendix A).

**Shapechanger:** The wererat acolyte can use its action to polymorph into a rat-humanoid hybrid or into a giant rat, or back into its true humanoid form. Its statistics, other than its size, are the same in each form. Any equipment it is wearing or carrying isn't transformed. It reverts to its true form if it dies.

**Keen Smell:** The wererat acolyte has advantage on Wisdom (Perception) checks that rely on smell.

**Spellcasting:** The wererat acolyte is a 1st-level spellcaster. Its spellcasting ability is Wisdom (spell save DC 12, +4 to hit with spell attacks). The wererat acolyte has the following cleric spells prepared (an asterisked spell is from appendix B):

- Cantrips (at will): *guidance, mending, resistance*
- 1st level (3 slots): *command, necrotic wave,* *shield of faith*

### ACTIONS

**Multiattack (Humanoid or Hybrid Form Only):** The wererat acolyte makes two attacks, only one of which can be a bite.

**Bite (Rat or Hybrid Form Only):** *Melee Weapon Attack:* +4 to hit, reach 5 ft., one target. *Hit:* 4 (1d4 + 2) piercing damage. If the target is a humanoid, it must succeed a DC 11 Constitution saving throw, or be cursed with wererat lycanthropy.

**Dagger (Humanoid or Hybrid Form Only):** *Melee or Ranged Weapon Attack:* +4 to hit, reach 5 ft. or range 20/60 ft.), one target. *Hit:* 4 (1d4 + 2) piercing damage.

## FIRE MEPHIT

*Small elemental, neutral evil*

**AC:** 12

**Hit Points:** 22 (5d6 + 5)

**Speed:** 30 ft., fly 30 ft.

| STR | DEX | CON | INT | WIS | CHA |
| --- | --- | --- | --- | --- | --- |
| 9 (-1) | 15 (+2) | 12 (+1) | 7 (-2) | 10 (+0) | 10 (+0) |

**Skills:** Stealth +4

**Damage Vulnerabilities:** cold

**Damage Immunities:** fire, poison

**Condition Immunities:** poisoned

**Senses:** darkvision 60 ft., passive perception 10

**Languages:** Ignan

**Challenge:** 1/2 (100 XP)

**Death Burst:** When the fire mephit dies, it explodes in a burst of flames. Each creature within 5 feet of it must make a DC 11 Dexterity saving throw, taking 6 (2d4 + 1) fire damage on a failed save, or half as much on a successful one.

**False Appearance:** While the fire mephit remains motionless, it is indistinguishable from an ordinary fire.

**Innate Spellcasting (1/Day):** The fire mephit can innately cast *burning hands* (spell save DC 10), requiring no components. Its innate spellcasting ability is Charisma.

*ACTIONS*

**Claws:** *Melee Weapon Attack:* +4 to hit, reach 5 ft., one creature. *Hit:* 4 (1d4 + 2) slashing damage plus 2 (1d4) fire damage.

**Fire Breath (Recharge 6):** The fire mephit exhales a 15-foot cone of fire. Each creature in the area must make a DC 11 Dexterity saving throw, taking 5 (2d4) fire damage on a failed save, or half as much damage on a successful one.

*This imp-like humanoid has a fiery, lithe body, enshrouded within an inky smoke cloud. It has an exaggerated pointy nose with flaring nostrils, and oversized ears spewing flames.*

## AWARDING EXPERIENCE

If the characters defeat the skeletal rat swarm, divide 50 XP among them. If the characters defeat Illyana, divide 450 XP among them. If the characters defeat the fire mephit, divide 100 XP among them. If the characters locate and avoid the pit trap, divide 50 XP among them.

---

### WERERAT IMMUNITIES

Illyana is a difficult challenge for a party of 1st-level characters. Even if they don't have magic or silvered weapons, they can still use spells or good old-fashioned grappling to neutralize their foe. In addition, the silver bullets in area 1, the magic dagger in area 2, the scrolls in area 5, and the magic oil in area 8f would all be very useful to overcome her immunities to non-magical damage sources.

---

## AREA 8 – NATURAL CAVERNS

When the characters enter these natural winding passages, read or paraphrase the following:

*These passages are clearly natural, and as such the walls, ceiling, and floor are rough and uneven. These passages are somewhat danker, and lack illumination.*

These are indeed natural caverns created centuries ago via water erosion. The ceiling height and width of the corridor vary in places, requiring occasional stooping or squeezing to get through. As depicted on the map, these corridors meander for some distance under the keep. Eventually, they lead to an exit (area 8h), but if the GM is so inclined, this is the perfect location to expand the scope of this adventure with additional corridors, chambers, and encounters.

Illyana uses these passages to enter and leave the keep unnoticed. She is well aware of all the dangers (some are simple traps she added), and has created a safe route as depicted on the map. It requires a successful DC 14 Wisdom (Survival) check to find this well-used route. At each intersection, have the tracker make the check again to follow the correct path.

There are many small encounter areas throughout these passages, as described below.

## A - GIANT BLIGHT RAT LAIR

The passage ends at roughly circular 10-foot-diameter chamber. The floor is covered with rotting fabric, tapestries, burlap, and organic debris such as twigs, leaves, and even some soft dirt. This area is the lair of nine **giant blight rats**. The giant blight rats pursue fleeing characters.

For every 10 minutes the characters spend searching through the nest, there is a 50% chance of catching the disease carried by these creatures (DC 10 Constitution save; check for each character). But for every 10 minutes spent searching, roll once on the following table to determine what is found.

| 2D6 | Item(s) Found |
| --- | --- |
| 2 | *Potion of healing* (only 1) |
| 3-4 | 3d6 sp and 1d6 gp |
| 5-8 | Nothing |
| 9-10 | 1d4 ep and 1d6 gp |
| 11 | Silver ring set with jet (worth 55 gp) |
| 12 | *+1 arrow* with green fletching |

## GIANT BLIGHT RAT (9)

*Small beast, unaligned*

**AC:** 11

**Hit Points:** 9 (2d6 + 2)

**Speed:** 30 ft.

| STR | DEX | CON | INT | WIS | CHA |
| --- | --- | --- | --- | --- | --- |
| 7 (-2) | 13 (+1) | 13 (+1) | 2 (-4) | 10 (+0) | 4 (-3) |

**Senses** darkvision 60 ft., passive perception 10

**Languages:** -

**Challenge:** 1/8 (25 XP)

**Keen Smell:** The giant blight rat has advantage on Wisdom (Perception) checks that rely on smell.

**Pack Tactics:** The giant blight rat has advantage on an attack roll against a creature if at least one of the giant blight rat's allies is within 5 feet of the creature and the ally isn't incapacitated.

### ACTIONS

**Bite:** *Melee Weapon Attack:* +3 to hit, reach 5 ft., one target. *Hit:* 3 (1d4 + 1) piercing damage. If the target is a creature, it must succeed on a DC 10 Constitution saving throw or contract a disease. After an onset of 12 hours, and until the disease is cured, the target suffers disadvantage on all Dexterity-based attacks and saving throws from muscle fatigue and soreness. The target's maximum hit points are reduced by 2 (1d4) every 24 hours, and hit points can only be regained via magical means. If the target's hit point maximum drops to 0 as the result of this blight, the target dies.

### AWARDING EXPERIENCE

For each giant blight rat the characters defeat, divide 25 XP among them. If the characters find the potion or the magic arrow, divide 25 XP among them.

## B - GREEN SLIME PATCH

Just south of this intersection is a small patch of **green slime** (Dungeon Master's Guide, p. 105) on the ceiling. Due to the low ceiling, the characters can spot this hazard with a successful DC 18 Wisdom (Perception) check if actively searching. Otherwise, it drops on the first character to pass underneath. At the start of each of its next turns, the target suffers 5 (1d10) acid damage until cleaned off. Cleaning off the slime takes an action. Green slime causes 11 (2d10) acid damage to any wooden or metal objects, so any nonmagical tool used to scrap off the slime will likely be destroyed.

### AWARDING EXPERIENCE

If the characters notice and avoid the green slime, divide 50 XP among them.

## C - ROCK FALL TRAP

At this intersection is a tripwire rigged to spring a simple trap. The tripwire can be detected with a successful DC 13 Wisdom (Perception) check. The trap can be disabled with a successful DC 12 Dexterity check using thieves' tools, or it can be simply avoided if found. If triggered, it releases a gray tarp suspended on the ceiling. The tarp is holding about 120 pounds of jagged rocks which dump onto the creature that triggered the tripwire. That target must make a successful DC 13 Dexterity saving throw, suffering 7 (2d6) bludgeoning damage on a failure, or half that amount on a success.

## Awarding Experience

If the characters notice and avoid the trap, divide 25 XP among them.

## D - SPRING-LOADED BAR TRAP

At this intersection is a tripwire rigged to spring a simple trap. The tripwire can be detected with a successful DC 13 Wisdom (Perception) check. The trap can be disabled with a successful DC 13 Dexterity check using thieves' tools, or it can be simply avoided. If triggered, it releases a spring-loaded wooden board painted gray and studded with caltrops. The board swings 4 feet off the ground, so it might harmlessly pass over a short halfling or gnome. The target that tripped the wire needs to make a successful DC 14 Dexterity saving throw, or suffer 3 (1d4 + 1) bludgeoning damage and 4 (1d6 + 1) piercing damage from impact. A successful save indicates the target ducked under the board in time and suffers no damage. Triggering the trap renders it useless.

## Awarding Experience

If the characters notice and avoid the trap, divide 25 XP among them.

## E - ROCK SNAKE LAIR

As the characters pass by the corridor that leads to this dead end, they notice flickering illumination. The illumination comes from a torch enchanted with a *continual flame* spell, discarded here by Illyana to lure enemies into the snake's lair. The torch is worth 50 gp.

Coiled into a recess of the wall is a **giant poisonous rock snake**, nearly 8 feet long. Due to its hiding spot and its textured gray-brown skin, a character's opposed Wisdom (Perception) check is at disadvantage to the giant poisonous rock snake's Dexterity (Stealth) check (which is at advantage due to its Stone Camouflage trait). If not noticed, the giant poisonous rock snake attacks with surprise. If reduced to 5 or fewer hit points, it retreats deeper into the recess in the wall and discontinues attacks unless further provoked.

## GIANT POISONOUS ROCK SNAKE

*Medium beast, unaligned*

**AC:** 13 (natural armor)
**Hit Points:** 13 (2d8 + 4)
**Speed:** 30 ft.

| STR | DEX | CON | INT | WIS | CHA |
|---|---|---|---|---|---|
| 10 (+0) | 14 (+2) | 14 (+2) | 2 (-4) | 11 (+0) | 3 (-4) |

**Skills:** Perception +2, Stealth +4
**Senses:** blindsight 20 ft., passive perception 12
**Languages:** -
**Challenge:** 1/4 (50 XP)

**Stone Camouflage:** The giant poisonous rock snake has advantage on Dexterity (Stealth) checks made to hide while in rocky terrain.

### ACTIONS

**Bite:** *Melee Weapon Attack:* +4 to hit, reach 10 ft., one target. *Hit:* 5 (1d6 + 2) piercing damage, and the target must make a DC 11 Constitution saving throw, taking 8 (2d6 + 1) poison damage on a failed save, or half as much on a successful one.

*This 8-foot-long snake has gray-brown skin adorned with textured knobby protrusions. Its forked black tongue flickers from a wide mouth situated on a triangular head.*

## Awarding Experience

If the characters defeat the giant poisonous rock snake, divide 50 XP among them.

## F - CAVE MORAY LAIR

At this area the corridor widens to an oval-shaped cyst. Along the north wall is a crack about 2 to 3 feet wide, running nearly to the ceiling. Hiding in this crack is a **cave moray**, the top predator in these natural caves. Unless noticed with a successful Wisdom (Perception) check opposed by the cave moray's Dexterity (Stealth) check, it attacks with surprise and utilizes its Lightning Strike trait. Once it hits a creature, it latches on and pulls the creature to its lair (see below). If the target is Medium-sized, it suffers 2 (1d4) bludgeoning damage each turn as the cave moray forces its meal through the tiny passage. If reduce to 8 or fewer hit points, the cave moray releases a grappled target, and retreats to its lair to lick its wounds.

A Tiny or Small creature can pass through here, but a Medium-sized creature needs to squeeze. This crack winds its way for about 18 feet before arriving at a round chamber perhaps 6 feet in diameter, but with a ceiling only 5 feet high. This chamber is the lair of the cave moray and even though it's a Large creature, its serpentine-like body can squeeze through the access crack. Inside its lair are numerous bones (some appear to be humanoid), the half-eaten body of Garan, organic debris (tree limbs, twigs, leaves, and the like), and several smooth rocks situated in a circle. Spending at least 10 minutes searching reveals an assortment of coins (41 sp, 7 ep, 12 gp, and 2 pp), and a small metal flask in the shape of a dryad. Two tiny emeralds serve as the dryad's eyes, and the flask is worth 175 gp. It holds one application of *oil of magic weapon* (see appendix A).

## CAVE MORAY

*Large beast, unaligned*

**AC:** 15 (natural armor)

**Hit Points:** 30 (4d10 + 8)

**Speed:** 15 ft.

| STR | DEX | CON | INT | WIS | CHA |
| --- | --- | --- | --- | --- | --- |
| 14 (+2) | 15 (+2) | 14 (+2) | 6 (-2) | 12 (+1) | 4 (-3) |

**Skills:** Perception +3, Stealth +4

**Senses:** darkvision 60 ft., passive perception 13

**Languages:** -

**Challenge:** 1 (200 XP)

**Drag:** The cave moray can use a bonus action on its turn to drag a grappled creature up to 5 feet.

**Keen Smell:** The cave moray has advantage on Wisdom (Perception) checks that rely on smell.

**Lightning Strike:** If a cave moray surprises a target, it gets advantage on its first attack roll.

### ACTIONS

**Bite:** *Melee Weapon Attack:* +4 to hit, reach 10 ft., one target. *Hit:* 7 (2d4 + 2) piercing damage. If the target is a Medium or smaller creature, it is grappled (escape DC 12). Until this grapple ends, the target is restrained, and the cave moray can't bite another target.

*This creature has a thick, serpentine bulky body with a dark purple hide, perhaps 9 feet long. Its smooth head sports large black eyes, and a triangular maw lined with piercing teeth.*

## AWARDING EXPERIENCE

If the characters defeat the cave moray, divide 200 XP among them.

## G - GHOULSTIRGE LAIR

At this location, there is a 1-foot-wide crack near the ceiling that eventually leads to the outside, high along the cliff face on the keep's western side. A Tiny creature can fit through the crack and use it to exit the caves.

Roosting on the ceiling in this area are three **ghoulstirges**. If disturbed, they attack. Being mindless undead, they attack until destroyed. If one (or more) becomes satiated on blood, it detaches and flees through the crack in the ceiling. A ghoulstirge is created when a mundane stirge feeds on a ghoul, becoming infused with necrotic energy. The stirge dies a few hours later, but then within 24 hours, it reanimates as an undead pest with a paralyzing bite.

## GOULSTIRGE (3)

*Tiny undead, unaligned*

**AC:** 13 (natural armor)

**Hit Points:** 7 (2d4 + 2)

**Speed:** 10 ft., fly 30 ft.

| STR | DEX | CON | INT | WIS | CHA |
| --- | --- | --- | --- | --- | --- |
| 4 (-3) | 15 (+2) | 13 (+1) | 2 (-4) | 10 (+0) | 4 (-3) |

**Senses:** darkvision 60 ft., passive perception 10

**Languages:** -

**Challenge:** 1/4 (50 XP)

### ACTIONS

**Paralyzing Blood Drain:** *Melee Weapon Attack:* +4 to hit, reach 5 ft., one creature. *Hit:* 4 (1d4 + 2) piercing damage plus 1 necrotic damage, and the ghoulstirge attaches to the target. If the target is a creature other than an elf or undead, it must succeed on a DC 10 Constitution saving throw or become paralyzed for 1 minute. The target can repeat the saving throw at the end of each of its turns, ending the effect on itself with a success.

While attached, the ghoulstirge doesn't attack. Instead, at the start of each of the ghoulstirge's turns, the target takes 1 necrotic damage and loses 4 (1d4 + 2) hit points due to blood loss.

The ghoulstirge can detach itself by spending 5 feet of its movement. It does so, flying off to digest its meal, after it drains 12 hit points of blood from the target or the target dies. A creature, including the (non-paralyzed) target, can use its action to detach the ghoulstirge, although this causes 1 point of slashing damage to the target.

*This horrid creature has sickly gray skin with open sores, pockmarked with tufts of black hair. It appears to be a cross between a large bat and a bloated mosquito. It has dirt-encrusted talons, milky-white eyes, and a black proboscis.*

## AWARDING EXPERIENCE

For each ghoulstirge the characters defeat, divide 50 XP among them.

## H - THE WAY OUT

A gray tarp conceals this corridor, although if a character is tracking the footprints, they find it automatically. Otherwise, it requires a successful DC 12 passive Perception check to locate. Beyond is a 25-foot corridor that apparently ends. But a quick examination reveals a stone that can be easily moved to provide exit. The exit is a ledge barely 5 feet wide, located on the cliff face, about 250 feet above the ground. Illyana maintains a gray silk rope with knots hidden in a nearby recess to scale the cliff. It requires a successful DC 14 Wisdom (Perception) check to find the rope. One end of the rope is fastened to a metal bar sunk into the rock, and it can be used to make the descent safer.

Also located in the corridor behind another gray tarp is a small alcove. This alcove is automatically located when approached because it contains a wooden cage holding six cooing pigeons. These are carrier pigeons used by Illyana to send messages to the hidden temple, and to a local band of brigands that lair in a nearby forest that typically waylay her marks for eventual delivery to the temple's sacrificial altar.

Next to the cage is a wooden chest with iron bands and a locked padlock. Illyana has the only key, or the lock can be picked with a successful DC 17 Dexterity check using thieves' tools. Inside the chest are two normal daggers, a full wineskin, and a teak scroll tube (worth 45 gp) holding seven sheets of parchment (one ripped into small pieces). In addition, in an electrum bowl (worth 85 gp) there are 12 small leather harnesses suitable to attach to either a carrier pigeon or a rat. Each harness holds a hollow bamboo tube suitable to place a small piece of parchment. A concealed bottom in the chest can be discovered with a successful DC 18 Wisdom (Perception) check. Inside are 11 gold trade bars (each worth 50 gp), and a pouch of six pearls (each worth 100 gp). This represents Illyana's ill-gotten gains from betraying innocent travelers.

## CONCLUDING THE ADVENTURE

At the GM's discretion, Illyana can make her last stand at area 8h. Or, she can simply flee in advance of the characters' arrival, and become a reoccurring villain. She flees to the hidden temple of chaos in the wilderness to heal up and gather a few supplies. Although her primary goal is to set up her operation again to serve her god, she holds a grudge against the characters and would not pass up an opportunity to exact some revenge. This would likely not be a direct assault, but instead hit-and-run tactics, or subtle acts via intermediaries.

Astute players might think to use the carrier pigeons to their advantage by luring the recipients to revealing their location and/or motives. This requires a successful DC 15 Charisma (Deception) check to write a convincing message. The GM may waive this check if the characters actually pen a creative message and present it. Secondly, a successful DC 15 Wisdom (Animal Handling) check is required to attach the message securely and convince the pigeon to deliver the missive. Success grants information on either the hidden temple of chaos, or the secret bandit hideout often employed to capture and transport victims. Should the characters confront the bandits in their hideout and rout them, the local garrison would likely provide a monetary reward if proof can be provided.

## Awarding Experience

If the characters succeed in using the pigeons to discover the location of the bandit lair, divide 100 XP among them. If the characters succeed in using the pigeons to discover the location of the temple of chaos, divide 150 XP among them.

# Appendix A: New Magic Items

## Elemental Shard

*Wondrous item, uncommon*

This crystal appears to be a shard hewn from a larger gem. An *elemental shard* is created when the manufacture of an *elemental gem* (Dungeon Master's Guide, pp. 167-168) fails, and the gem used fragments into several shards. Sometimes these shards contain a minor mote of elemental energy based on the type of gem it originated from.

When you use an action to break the shard (typically by throwing it against a hard surface), a single mephit is summoned as if you had cast *conjure minor elementals*. The type of mephit summoned depends on the type of gem from which the shard came.

## Oil of Magic Weapon

*Potion, uncommon*

This viscid oil has a silvery sheen. The oil can coat one normal humanoid-sized weapon (such as a mace or a longsword) or 10 pieces of ammunition. Applying the oil takes 1 minute. For 1 hour, the coated item is magical and has a +1 bonus to attack and damage rolls.

# Appendix B: New Spell

## Necrotic Wave

*1st-level necromancy*

**Casting Time:** 1 action
**Range:** Self (30-foot cone)
**Components:** V, S, M (a pinch of grave dirt)
**Duration:** Instantaneous

A wave of enervating necrotic energy sweeps out from you. Each creature in a 30-foot cone originating from you must make a Constitution saving throw. On a failed save, a creature takes 2d4 necrotic damage and is at disadvantage on all melee attacks and Strength-based skill checks and saves until the end of their next turn. On a successful save, the creature only suffers half damage.

**At Higher Levels:** When you cast this spell using a spell slot of 2nd level or higher, the damage increases by 2d4 for each slot level above 1st.